TAMING DESTRUCTION

DUTIFUL GODS

BOOK TWO

MELISSA BELL

BLURB

Destruction is the master of his realm, the creator of Natural Disasters from erupting volcano's to raging tsunamis, shattering earthquakes and devastating hurricanes.

Megan is a woman who has already lost everything, her mother, her father and the man she loved, the man she was supposed to spend her life with. Megan now stands to lose anything she has left, her family home and her mothers craft shop. There is a cyclone, hovering off the coast, getting closer and closer by the minute.

What will happen when Destruction meets Megan? Will he destroy her, too?

*This Book is dedicated to **Jordin Thiele***

***Jordin Thiele** you are my light, my life and without you I would not be able to pursue my dream of writing. Your understanding and faith in me astound me beyond words. I love you*

***You**, the world of readers who have discovered reading Book's; No matter what time of day or night it is in your part of the world. The time you take to read this Book is just as valuable as the time it takes to write it.*

***Sharon Higgs** – The first person to buy Destiny's Fate and leave an Awesome review.*

CONTENT WARNING

The following book contains Adult (18+) Themes, including graphic sexual scenes and language that may offend or disturb some readers.
All characters are fictional and portrayed as mature adults 18 years old and over.

ACKNOWLEDGMENTS

Editor
EMGARRY

CHAPTER 1

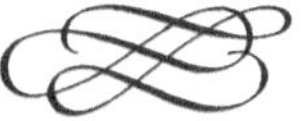

Destruction entered his realm, he returned the missing emblem to its location. His brother had a female; jealousy spiked deep within him.

He wanted a female, but he didn't dare touch a human, the thought terrified him. Everything he touched crumbled, like a brittle biscuit.

The only place safe for him was in his realm. That he could control, his surroundings protected by his mother's bestowal. However, if he left his home, he couldn't touch a single thing without destroying it.

He wanted to know how he could find a

woman strong enough to make his own in all ways.

Disheartened, he focused on the enormity of his role as Destruction.

He often reflected on why he had been given this realm, why not Dream, or Death. The thought that land and life were to be lost left him cold and lonely on the inside. That's why he needed to find his mate, his good to his bad, because that's how he saw himself. Nothing good ever came out of his divination.

He was growing increasingly unhappy with his role in the big picture; not that he had ever been happy about it to start with.

He turned his back on the map's surface, storming out of the room. He knew better than to touch anything in the mood he was presently garnishing. He'd be likely to wipe out the entire human population in one foul swipe of his power.

He needed to calm himself down. Maybe he needed some downtime. He couldn't remember the last time he'd actually slept. Minutes crept into hours, hours into days, days into weeks, and years. He was tired of it all, his faith in the universe had been all but destroyed.

He stormed into his bedroom and started to strip on his way to the shower. Maybe he could wash away some of the residue attached to his skin.

As he wrapped the towel round his hips, he left the bathroom and headed for his king-sized bed. Sitting down, he opened his side table drawer and removed the soft pouch of dream sand given to him by his brother. Not bothering to measure it, he lifted his thumb to his forehead and deposited a healthy dose between his brows, smudging upwards. Closing the pouch, he placed it back in the drawer, stood to drop his towel, and climbed into his bed silently praying that his dreams would be filled with something other than destruction.

MEGAN KNEW SHE HAD LIMITED TIME TO prepare for the cyclone steadily moving closer to the coastline with every passing hour. She had done her best to prepare her house. She'd packed everything worth keeping, which wasn't much, into the basement and sandbagged the door. Anything else would hopefully be covered by insurance and she had a little saved up in case of a rainy day. Her father had taught her that lesson as a kid. She'd packed most of her clothes into a couple of suitcases and loaded them into her old Toyota. Her father had been an emotionally cold man. He never said he loved her, but he gave her guidance and lessons. While other parents bought cars for their kids as they got their licenses, her dad helped her take out the finance. He spent three days searching for the right car, while she worked to earn the money to make payments on it. She had been eighteen at the time. He met her after work and the deal was done. She had paid off the car years ago, keeping it maintained. She was reliable even if she wasn't pretty. She had a moment of sadness, her father had disconnected after her mother's death, not just from her, but from life in general. She had laid him to rest within a matter of months after her mother. She had moved back into the family home, and had taken over the running of her mother's shop.

She was still at odds as to whether she was going to keep either or both. She had a flair for her mother's passion, but as life had thrown curve balls her direction at every turn, her faith had been shaken not stirred. She had her own emotional cyclone going on inside her heart and her head. She felt she was standing in the eye of a storm, being pulled in different directions.

With time closing in on her fast before the impending cyclone proceeded, closing off roads and evacuation from the area, she needed to get her shit happening. Like now as in yesterday. With her car loaded, she headed to her mother's shop. She couldn't afford to lose the last pieces of her mother.

The sheets of rain made it hard to see, accompanied by the strong winds trying to push her off the road, making the short distance to the shop exhausting.

Parking her car in the back carpark, she figured it would be somewhat protected by the surrounding block of shops. She locked the door and headed out to the front of the shop.

She been thinking about a plan of action so she could be in and out as quick as possible. The easiest solution being too quickly pack stuff into boxes from the storeroom. Opening the door, she raced in not thinking to prop the door open until she heard it slam shut. "Fuck!"

CHAPTER 2

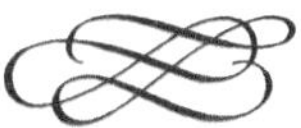

Megan started pacing. She needed to figure a way out of here, before things became even worse than just bad.

She had lost her faith in the powers that be. Her mother had tried to encourage her with teachings. It hadn't been her mother's fault that the boy she had fallen in love with as child would grow into a man of war. He had been two years older than her and the day after his eighteenth birthday, he had enlisted in the army. She had only seen him once more after that, she thought, as a tear rolled down her cheek. Shaun had come home for his mother's funeral, after which he had kissed her deeply, asking her to wait for him. He promised to come home and make a life with her, which never happened. He died in an ambush on a scouting mission. A piece of her died that same day; he was supposed to come home to find that she had waited. He was supposed come home and be her partner in life, but after many nights crying for what she'd lost, she woke up after a dream to realise he wasn't coming back no matter how many tears she cried. She had straightened her spine, held her head high, and decided to live for him. He wouldn't be her partner in life, and she wouldn't be his in death.

She had built walls of ice around her heart. It was the way it was then and still is now, almost ten years later.

She started looking through the shelves in the storeroom, not having much faith that it would work, but needing to try anyway.

DESTRUCTION WAS DREAMING OF THE MOST exquisite female he had ever seen. She was built like a real woman; tall and strong boned, curves that could fill his large hands with softness. She had hair like angry fire light, curling down her back. She had just taken a band from her wrist and pulled it in a bunch on top of her head, making his finger itch to release it. He wanted to feel it between his fingers, to see if it was as soft to the touch as it appeared.

She was busy collecting items from the shelves in a small but tidy room. There were a number of items on a stone bench on the floor. He could make out a goblet, a dagger, an urn with little leaves, bottles of oil. She removed all her clothes, picked up a bag of salt and made a circle. The four chunks of crystal she placed to make four corners. She took the oil from the altar and anointed her flawless skin, then removed the band, allowing her hair to fall softly down her oiled body. She tossed the band where her cloths rested. She waved her hand over a candle and nothing happened, she sighed.

Rubbing her hands together she said, "Come on Megan, you're supposed to be a seventh generation witch." She placed her hand on her knees, taking deep, relaxing breaths. She felt the flicker of light in her solar plexus and she focused her energy on it. Collected a memory from her mother's teachings and letting the ball of light glow. Bright white light started to radiate through her body until it felt like her entire body was tingling with its essence, its power. Slowly lifting her hand, she waved it over the candle as the wick flamed to life. She felt a calm override her senses. She exhaled slowly, not realising she had been anxiously holding her breath.

She was trying not to let her focus waver, as the sound of the wind and rain steadily grew stronger outside. Right now, fear and self-doubt were not an option. The negative energy would interfere with the power needed to get her out of this situation alive, all be it in one piece. Her mind was another matter altogether, though. Her mother had always been a little bat shit crazy but in her own lovable way.

"Focus Megan, focus!" Her mother would have said. She said a little a prayer to her mother for strength and guidance. She opened her eyes and lifted her face, picturing the white-robed deity in her mind, and started to chant.

Destruction felt as if someone had sucker-punched him in the stomach. When she finally looked up, he saw ocean blue eyes. He could barely breathe; she was breathtakingly beautiful. The candlelight illuminating her skin, making it glow. He had been mesmerised as she had stripped her clothing off.

He knew nothing about this female other than her name, Megan. He felt tingles in places he wanted to feel her strong hands, as she had spoken to herself. He had felt her voice trickle through him, waking every cell of his being. One thought coming hard and fast, loud and clear, "Mine!" He had to have her; he didn't care about the how, he didn't care the when. No, that was a lie. He'd waited too long for this moment to let it go. His body needed her like he needed his next breath. His entire body was humming so strong it was becoming painful. His muscles starving for blood, his breathing heavy, he recognised all his common sense had vacated south. His dick so hard he could hammer nails into stone.

He needed to wake up, he needed to find her. What then? He couldn't touch her, she was human. If he was to slide his hands over her alabaster skin, she would bruise. It would leave her broken, maybe even dead.

Disheartened at the thought of never being able to touch her, kiss her or be inside her, he concentrated on the ritual she was performing.

CHAPTER 3

Cosmo felt the call. She didn't recognise the energy but it did possess a familiarity to it. The power was fragile, newly tested, yet old.

Did she really want to waste her time and energy on her curiosity or was the fragrance of the petals floating in her hot bath louder?

Balancing naked with her toe poised to enter the sweet smelling tub, the energy flared. "Oh, alright already!" she muttered, placing her foot back on the floor. Waving her hands down her torso, she donned her white gown, and vanished.

She reappeared in a tiny room with a

young woman on her knees in front of an altar. She could sense the turmoil inside the women, as well as the surging energy of her son. The kerfuffle going on outside had Destruction's energy all over it.

She understood this female's destiny was laid out on the altar at her feet. Ok then, she thought, let's get this show on the road as they say.

The look of surprise in the woman's face said a lot. She had the knowledge but not the experience. Hmmm, interesting she thought, this might not be a total waste of time after all.

She started by asking, "What's your name child?"

"Megan," she whispered. She gave a little cough to clear her throat, and tried again. "Megan Delaney, I am the seventh of the Delaney line. Daughter of Meghan, daughter of Meagen, daughter..." She trailed off as Cosmo interrupted, "Yes, yes, I know who the Delaney daughters are. I do not recall much after the passing of your mother however."

"Yes, my Lady, and for that I am eternally

embarrassed and beg your forgiveness?" She was not beyond begging if it came to her life. She was not ready to die for something a simple apology could rectify.

"Alright, so why did you falter child? Why did you step away from your faith?" Cosmo asked, wanting the details before she could accept Megan's apology.

Megan's face took on a sad, reflective look. Cosmo waited and watched as Megan processed and constructed her reply. She finally answered, "I lost the love of my life, the man I would have married and had children with."

Cosmo pondered Megan's answer, which made her wonder at the term Megan had used. "Lost, you say? To what form of the word are you referring to?" She patiently waited for Megan's response.

A single tear trailed down her cheek, as she explained. "He was killed while deployed overseas."

Cosmo placed a gentle hand on Megan's cheek, using her thumb to brush away the stray tear. "I know that the universe is sometimes a harsh place to exist in, but when you stray from your beliefs, it makes things even harder. As I see, you have come to the understanding of your wrongs and have reconnected with your heritage. I will, this time, listen to your plea. Now take a deep breath, clear your thoughts and make your request of me."

"I need your help to get away from here, the storeroom door shut and I have no way to open it from the inside. There is a cyclone coming and is very nearly upon us or, should I say, me. Will you please get me out of here?" She begged, almost frantically. She was well aware that if Cosmo said no, the balance of her life sat teetering on the edge of life and death.

Cosmo thought about all Megan had said. She had made her mind up that she would help Megan, just not in the way Megan thought.

Cosmo grasped Megan's hand before she could argue. "Take my hand, child,"

CHAPTER 4

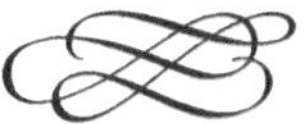

Destruction woke up with a start; the energy in his realm had shifted. He climbed out of bed, grabbed his towel, and started toward the door. He'd taken two steps when he noticed himself proudly standing harder than ever. Damn. He quickly pushed his legs into a pair of leathers and very cautiously positioned himself to conceal his hard on as best he could.

He stormed out the room in search of the intruder. He pulled up short in the doorway of his library. Standing there, in full naked glory, was the woman of his dreams, literally. Butt naked. He looked behind himself and surveyed the room to catch sight of anyone else. Nope, he thought, ok, I'm still dreaming, right?

He quietly approached the redhead beauty, his hand extending towards the flames captured within her fiery hair. As his fingers brushed a predominant curl, his female spun low, laying her shoulder into his stomach. At the same time, she wrapped her hand in a hunk of his leather pants. He hit the floor with a crash so hard the room shook. "What the fuck?" Dreams don't have a woman kicking your ass. Her moves had taken him completely by surprise. He had recovered just enough grasp her arm. With the forward momentum, she landed on top of him with a shocked squeak.

Her naked chest landed against his. She pushed herself up, trying to free herself from the stranger. As her hair trailed her path of retreat, Destruction felt himself harden to the point of pain. Fuck, she felt good and smelt even better.

Megan had no idea who this guy was but damn he was huge. The enormous ridge in his pants said so, ain't no lie about that. She took a shuddering breath, placed a hand on his stomach, and stood up. "Who are you?" She watched a sly smile twitch at the corner of the most handsome man she had ever seen. His hair long and black with an unruly kink to it, accentuated the hard angles and strong lines of his features. Her heart rate increased, "What are you looking at me like that for? Stop it! You jumped me. I don't like people sneaking up on me."

Still standing over Destruction, Megan placed her hands on her hips. She closed her eyes, before yelling, "Fuck me, this isn't a dream and I'm naked, like really? Fuck my life sideways on days like today!"

She lifted her head to the ceiling and muttered, "You could have given me something to wear. Where the hell am I anyway?"

Destruction was still lying on the floor between Megan's legs, her body on full display. He could hear her asking something but his tongue was glued to the roof of his mouth. Right along with his cognitive functions being squashed into leathers three sizes too damn small all of a sudden.

Megan brought him back to the here

and now by placing her foot on the inner crease of his hip; cognitive thought reactivated instantly. "Huh? What were you saying?" pushing himself up. Well the view was good down there but this was working for him too.

His eyes were following her plump pussy with the barest hint of red re-growth. She was naked, in the full sense of the word, naked. His tongue had managed to remove itself from the roof of his mouth, but now had him licking his lips suddenly thirsty.

She knocked on the top of his head with a knuckle, "Dah, up here big guy," she said as she moved away. Obviously his brain was suffering high blood pressure at the moment, judging from the bulge in between his legs. If those pants were any tighter, he would have an aneurysm.

She turned on her heel and stormed out of the room. She had no idea where the fuck she was. She entered what looked to be a bedroom, looking round she found the dresser drawers. Opening and closing a couple of drawers, she found what she was looking for. "Perfect!" She said, throwing the black shirt over her head and depositing her arms through the sleeves. She looked down to see it reach just above her knee; he was bigger than huge. She gave a sarcastic giggle, just as he walked into the room. He stood there for second, his chest puffing up at how good she looked in his shirt. With a puzzled look he asked, "What's tickling you?"

She smirked and replied, "The bigger they are, the harder they fall." She laughed, finally adding and "You're massive, and I landed you on your ass. Who would have thought there was so much truth in an old wives' tale?"

Destruction moved past Megan to reach into a drawer to snatch a pair of sweats. He couldn't think properly while his dick was being suffocated. He walked into the bathroom, closing the door. Removing his leathers, he stood in front of the mirror looking at his cock, acknowledging it had never been this demanding before.

His hand was drawn to it magnetically. His fingers had just banded its girth when the door burst open.

"Oh my god, what are you doing?" Megan exclaimed.

His eyes met hers in the mirror. As he replied, his hand started to work with a slow glide toward the tip. His other hand lifted to run his thumb over the head to smear the bead of seed, in a blatant dare.

"Shouldn't I be asking you, what do you think you're doing? This is my bathroom and the door was shut. Now, either you can back away or you can help me," he said with a smirk.

Megan blushed. She had never seen a real life one, up close and personal before. Sure, she had wanted to see Shaun's so bad she ached, but then he'd never come home to claim her. He'd asked her to wait for him, so she'd waited. Now she was a twenty-eight year old virgin. She wasn't frigid, she just hadn't met anyone worth touching in an intimate way. She just hadn't wanted any man to remind her what she could have had with Shaun or what she'd missed out on by gifting it to just a one night stand. What now? She couldn't think straight while he was challenging her.

Megan knew she should leave, she just had no idea why she didn't. She found herself licking her lips, her brain had gone south of his navel. Her feet had taken root on the cold tiles of the bathroom floor. Her breathing became heavy and her face was starting to feel sunburnt. She didn't want to even try to label that.

All that came out of her mouth was, "I, um, I." All of a sudden, he was there, right in her face. His bare chest barely touching her, his hardness against her stomach. His hand sliding gently into her hair, he moaned as he inhaled her scent.

He tilted her head up as his lips brushed

hers lightly. As she gasped, he made to withdraw, he didn't want to hurt her. Her hands moved of their own volition. He inhaled sharply as he felt her hands on his hips. Damn, he couldn't breathe. He waited eagerly, wanting the softness of her skin on his body so badly he ached. His muscles started to twitch from the restrain he was using to not pick her up and bury himself deep inside her silken glove.

"Megan, I don't want to scare you or hurt you but I want you, I want to do things with you, to you and I'm pushing my limits of self-control here. However, I think until we know more about each other, you need to move away from me, now!" he said, trying to do the right thing. Again, he made to retreat, his cock throbbing in protest.

"No, I. I'm sorry, I shouldn't have come in. It's my fault, I've had one of the worst days of my life. I'm thinking this one is probably right up there next to number one."

Megan reluctantly turned and left the bathroom, closing the door as she went. She leaned her back against it, needing support for her shaking legs. After taking a few deep breaths, she carefully made her way to the bed. Suddenly feeling the exhaustion of the day's events, and her out of control body, she laid down. Her eyes growing heavy and she sunk into the blissful darkness of sleep as she heard the water in the shower start to run.

Destruction stood there staring at the closed door, torn between doing what was right and what his body was demanding of him. His body was screaming at him to claim his fiery female, but he ignored it. He could still feel her hands on him. It had taken all of his willpower to move away from her. He had to clench his fists to stop himself from reaching out to her as she walked away. He'd wanted to pull her into his arms, but he couldn't trust his strength not to hurt her.

He stepped into the shower. He made it as cold as he possibly could, to try and dissolve the need burning inside him. Minutes later, he knew the cruelly cold water was not going to change anything. He needed to ease the ache in his cock. He turned his back to the shower spray and soaped up his hand. Closing his eyes, his imagination took him back to when he was on his back with her naked atop him in the library. His hand started to stroke in long slow steady glides. He could see her knees straddling him, he wanted inside her hot spot more than his next breath. Her red curls flowing around her shoulders, tickling her puckered nipples. Her head thrown back, a gasp escaping her plump cherry lips as he slid inside. Her hips rotating to feed more of him inside her, her hands resting on his ribs to maintain balance as she began to increase the pace. His hand picking up the rhythm of his imagination. His own hips lifting off the floor to meet her impalement, he was close. He could only imagine the sounds she would make as she came for him. A growl worked its way from his chest, his eyes flew open as he watched his seed erupt from his bulbous head. He came so hard he used his hand to brace himself on the wall. He cleaned himself up, turned the shower off and stepped out, shaking.

As he dried himself off efficiently, he

knew he'd never wanted for anything so bad as his want for Megan. He knew that if he didn't have her, his response would be the beginning of Armageddon.

He stepped into his sweat pants, opened the door turned off the light and froze. With his heart pounding, he blinked twice to confirm he wasn't dreaming.

What was she doing here? Not that he was complaining, but he failed to see how she came to be here in his realm. Was it something to do with his dream about her? Damn! Sandy, I wonder if you know the potent kick that sand of yours has, he thought as he continued to watch the most beautiful woman he'd ever seen, sleeping in his bed. He was chuffed. It felt good and it felt right.

Not able to resist the sirens call of her red silken hair, he moved to the bed in a hypnotized state.

He wanted to touch its flames; the way they played on the curls made his fingers itch.

He lifted a curl, leaned in close and kissed her temple. He couldn't help himself. She was too much of a temptation.

Against his better judgement he moved to the vacant side of his king-size bed, he told himself, "There's plenty of room."

He lifted the sheets and climbed in, willing the lights off.

Sleep quickly overtook him as he listened to Megan's slow and steady breathing beside him, right where she belonged.

CHAPTER 6

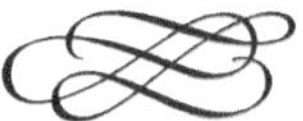

Destruction awoke to the sound of a female weeping. He could feel a soft body pushed up close to his side.

He turned to envelope her in his arms, trying to sooth her he whispered, "Its ok, I've got you." She was a perfect fit against his body, soft, where his body was hard. She smelt intoxicating, he wanted to kiss away her tears, turn her sobs into gasps of pleasure.

She whimpered in her sleep, "Don't leave me. I need you."

He replied softly in her ear as he rolled her over on her side, encompassing her with his mountainous body. "I'm not going anywhere. Shhh." She nestled further into his embrace. Her cheek rested against his chest. God she felt good, like she belonged in his arms. Everything in his world felt right for the first time in his existence. A peacefulness relaxed him back into slumber.

Megan woke for the first time in her life, feeling like she could breathe. She no longer felt weighed down by life's drama.

She moved to stretch, but was restricted by solid flesh, she was surrounded by it. For a moment she felt trapped, her cheek pressed against a smooth muscular chest. It smelt so good. She was past being tempted, as she licked her lips and tasted him.

Her body warmed, betraying the memory of Shaun. She should pull away. She pushed against his strong stomach, and froze when she realized the chest was no longer rising and falling. He was awake.

He moved with a speed someone of his size should not have possessed. He rolled her under him, and whispered in her ear, "If I didn't know any better Megan, I would think you were trying to escape from me."

She loved the way his lips touched her

ear sending electric tingles down her spine, and causing pools of wetness in her virginal walls. She was at odds with her body. She wanted to know about the secrets she'd denied herself for so long. She knew nothing about the guy awakening these sensations, making her feel. She was confused and she couldn't think straight as his hardness pressed against where she ached the most. She hated the fabric between them, but at the same time was thankful it was there.

He started to kiss his way from her ear, along her jaw, his lips gently brushing hers, as she gasped from the incredible sensations flooding her body, and his tongue penetrated her mouth tentatively.

All senses were lost as he enticed her to respond and she surrendered. For this moment in time, she didn't want to think about anything else. She'd be going home soon anyway.

He released her mouth and slowly kissed down her neck. As he ran the tip of his tongue around her puckered nipple, a fire ignited in her belly. She moaned, "More, I need more." He took her words as encouragement and took her nipple in his mouth. His lips wrapped around her nipple and he sucked as his tongue flickered over it. Her hips rose from the bed squirming for more pressure, her breathing growing heavy.

She felt her juices weeping from her aching pussy, her muscles clenching so tight it was almost painful.

She grabbed handfuls of his hair, to guide him to look at her, "I hurt, I can't, please do something, make it stop?" She begged, she needed more and she needed it now.

He moved down her stomach with kisses, he spread her legs wide around his shoulders. He wanted to be sure she was ready for him to claim her as his.

He'd never done this before, but that didn't mean he wasn't eager to try and make it good for her, with pleasures he'd only dreamt about.

He opened her plump lips and lowered his tongue to swipe along her cleft. Her natural oils exploded on his taste buds like ambrosia. He dove in deep, he didn't have time to worry about his inexperience. The sounds Megan was making spurred him on as she writhed around in pleasure.

He placed one hand on her hip to anchor her, as he fed a thick finger through her slick juices, sinking in slowly into her hot, wet channel.

Her finger nails dug into the bedding trying to gain purchase. "Argh, I, please, I need more." She begged, her head rolled from side to side. Her body was on fire, she couldn't take much more. "Do something, please?"

He inserted a second finger into her opening, and pushed her over the edge. "Yes, Yes, Gods Yes!" She could barely breath, she felt her muscles contracting and pulsing. She had touched herself before but it was never this intense.

As she staggered to catch her breath, he climbed back up her body and leaned down to kiss her. Her hands reached down between them to lower the band of his sweat pants, freeing his stiff cock. She wanted him inside her more than her next breath, "I want you, I need you, please?"

He did not take much to be convinced

him and there was no turning back. As her fingers wrapped around his hardness, he was guided into heaven.

His cock slick with Megan's juices centred at the entry, he held his breath as he slid the tip inside. Megan froze, as she braced herself for his invasion.

"Am I hurting you?" He asked.

"No. Wait! Stop!" She suddenly regained her senses enough to ask, "What's your name?"

He started to move away from her but she raised her hand to the base of his neck.

"No, don't, please. I just, oh hell, I've never given myself to a man before. I just want to know my first lover's name." she explained, as a tear ran down her cheek.

Destruction's mind spun with the realization that his woman was indeed just that; his. He'd never been with a woman before, but her plea was riding his possessive streak hard.

He held himself in check long enough to whisper his name, "Troy" against her lips as he pushed in hard, claiming her as his and his alone. His cock anchored at the neck of her cervix as he swallowed her gasp of pain.

He allowed her body to relax around him as he kissed her deeply, a silent vow of ownership. He would never let her go now. He would follow her to the ends of the earth and destroy anyone or anything that stood between them.

Her hips started to move of their own accord. He raised himself up on his elbows slowly sliding out until just the head was inside her entrance. "Am I hurting you?" again he asked.

She couldn't speak, shaking her head to indicate no. His hand slid down the outside of her breast and his thumb flicked her nipple, as his hand descended along her side to cup a handful of her ass. She tore her shirt off over her head. She needed skin to skin contact. No barriers, nothing between them.

He lifted her ass as he buried himself in her wet depths again and again. She fit him like a glove. She linked her ankles around his hips to spur him on, his pelvic ridge bumping her nub. He had her cresting the edge of orgasm when he lowered his head to suck her nipple; that's when she exploded. Wave after wave she crashed over the edge, her convulsing pussy took him with her. He lifted his head and as he buried himself deep inside, his hot seed flooded her.

She released her hold on him, her legs collapsed to the bed, boneless.

Her mind was as fucked as her body. She had been denying herself this pleasure for way too long.

How could she not want more? She thought as her body felt a loss as he slid free.

He rolled to her side not wanting to crush her with his weight. "Fuck, that was awesome," he said, wondering if he should mention this was his first time too. But thought better of it.

"So Troy, where is Cosmo?" she asked. She felt a little awkward now that the heat of the moment had passed.

Destruction looked around the room, feeling somewhat confused. He looked back at Megan and replied, "My mother isn't here, and this is my place."

"And where exactly is your place?" she asked, trying to figure out why Cosmo had brought her here.

Destruction knew things were not going how he expected them to. He was trying to figure things out himself.

"So you're saying my mother brought you here? How did she know?" he asked.

"Yes, that's what I said. She told me all I needed to save my life was here and then she was gone, poof!" she explained. "So if this is your place, exactly where is your place?"

Again he tried to dodge her question, "Where did you come from?"

"Ok big guy. I'm not answering any more questions until you answer mine. Where exactly am I?" she demanded, as she started to move away from him.

Things were turning pear-shaped faster than his brain could function. He took hold of her hand to stop her from getting away from him.

She stared at their joined hands before

lifting her eyes to meet his. "What is it you're not telling me? I'm getting a bad feeling about this!" she said with urgency.

"We really should get dressed for this. I can't think straight when you're naked, and for this conversation we need clothes." He pulled his sweats up as he passed her his shirt.

"You got anything decent to eat around here?" she asked as her stomach growled. She couldn't remember the last time she ate. She pulled the shirt over her head and stood from the bed.

Destruction instructed her, "Follow me. My sister usually leaves me a few treats. I'm sure there'll be something in the fridge."

She followed him. As they left the bedroom, she spared a look at the mussed up bedding. Her cheeks blushed as she felt their combined juices run down the inside of her leg.

A few steps down the hall she stated, "Wait, I need to get cleaned up. I'll only be a minute." As she turned, he moved faster than her eye could register.

She was spun around, her back bumped

against the wall. His strong arms caged her, his head lowered to her ear, "Do you find me repulsive? The thought of my seed being in you, on you distasteful?"

"No," She whispered.

"Good," he replied. "That's settled then. Follow me." Damn, he was all Neanderthal when he took control. He took her hand in his this time and started back towards the kitchen.

CHAPTER 8

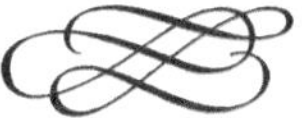

He led her to a stool at the kitchen bench, and pointed at it, "Park it. I'll organize something to eat." He walked to the fridge and removed a couple of beers. Sitting them on the bench, he opened one and offered it to Megan. She took it with a tilted salute, lifted it to her lips and downed a healthy swig. He hardened as he caught sight of her lips curved around the mouth of the bottle, and almost staggered as he watched the swallow move down her throat. "Come on, focus man!" he said under his breath.

Megan never thought that watching a

man prepare food for you could be so hot, even sexy and roast beef sandwiches had never tasted so good.

She hadn't had roast in a while. It was too much hassle to cook it for one person. "This is really good. Did you cook it yourself?"

"No, my sister Faith goes on a cooking frenzy every few days and brings it by. She lives alone and cooks up a storm when she's stressed about something. She says it's the one thing she can control."

She finished her sandwich and wanted to get down to the nitty gritty of things, "So, are you ready to talk? Maybe answer some of my questions? Or are we just going to continue to dance around with small talk avoiding the issues?"

She almost fell off her stool as he unleashed a smile that took her breath away, "Depends on what kind of dancing you had in mind?" he said with a wink.

She almost choked on the last mouthful of beer she'd taken.

Was he seriously hitting on her? Or was he deflecting, trying to distract her?

He took note of her response and walked around the kitchen bench to clear the dishes. "Ok, serious, it is then? Come with me. It's easier if I show you." He held out his hand, and then dropped it when she declined to take it.

He could feel the tension between them grow. He'd always struggled with who he was and what his duties were from the day Cosmo had handed them down to him on his twenty-first cycle.

He remembered being able to play with his siblings without injuring them. After that day, he had not been able to seek physical contact or comfort from any of them. He remembered his younger sister Faith's twenty-first cycle. He gave her a hug, but his embrace rendered her with three broken ribs. His mother repaired her injuries, but he'd seen the pain in her eyes and it haunted him ever since. She had, on numerous occasions, reminded him that it was not his fault and he was forgiven, but he would never forgive himself. He believed that her cooking for him was her way of offering him comfort and love. He had never reached out to anyone since. Not even in his own realm. He was even stronger there and he wouldn't chance injuring any of them again.

He led the way to his library and stood in front of his work. "You're in my house; it's the realm of Destruction." If she hated him after this disclosure then so be it, there was not much else he could do, as he refused to lie to her.

"I oversee all the destructive forces at work in the human realm." he explained, looking over his table map unable to meet her eyes.

She moved closer to the map, shocked yet curious about the way it worked. "So, you're saying the cyclone that was about to hit my home town was you're doing?"

"Yeah, along with the earthquakes in the US, the droughts in Africa, the tsunami in the Philippines. All of it is my doing. The wars are not my doing though. That's something else entirely. That's between Faith and Warh, they will never agree to just disagree. My brother Destiny has a hand in placing the people in the area that are meant to be there. My other brother Death collects the less fortunate souls that don't survive the aftermath. It's not safe for you to go home until the cyclone has passed." He was rambling, he knew it, but he was nervous for the first time in his long existence since he'd never had to explain his role before. He was praying to his mother that she knew what the hell she was doing when she sent Megan to his realm.

"Why did you tell me your name was Troy?" she whispered accusingly.

Would she have let him still touch her if she had known all this before? His head was beginning to pound from the stress.

"Troy is the name my brothers gave me. It's a nickname, short for Destroyer." He looked at her then, not able to help himself. She paled and took a step back.

The fleeting look of something in his eyes was but a flash and she wasn't certain if it had been there before. So quickly he had masked his expression that she couldn't even put a name to it. She needed to get away from here, fast. He held the power to destroy her. Her heart was beating so fast, panic over took her as she turned and ran.

He let her go. She obviously needed space and time to process what was going on.

CHAPTER 9

Megan ran as fast as her legs could carry her, out of the library and down the length of the hall. She reached a door at the end and grappled with the door knob praying it would be unlocked.

The door swung open as she checked over her shoulder to see if he was following. She stepped through and closed it.

"For fuck sake!" she cursed as her eyes failed to focus on anything. Her luck lately was so fucked up, trust her to step into a broom closet. She was feeling around for a light switch when a door on the other side of the room opened spewing light in. She spun around defensively to find a beautiful blond woman struggling with her hands full of baking trays.

"Crap, my day just keeps getting better and better," she said to herself.

The woman almost dropped the trays she was carrying.

She looked over her shoulder again and saw what looked to be another door, perhaps the way out. She opened the door and was closing it at when she heard the woman speak. "Hey? Who are you and what are you doing in here?"

She quickly closed the door behind her. This shit was getting weirder by the second. As she walked down the hall back to Troy's place, everything looked the same, but something was off. She saw pictures on the walls she didn't remember seeing before.

Now she was getting pissed, this was all too fucking confusing. She just wanted to go home, to her normal, boring, lonely life, thank you very much. Ok, so maybe minus the lonely.

Megan suddenly saw the woman from the pictures standing in front of her with a baby resting on her hip.

Yep, she thought, sure would hate to break the pattern.

Zandra laughed, "You come through that door?" She pointed down the hall behind Megan.

"It's all good, I'm not one of them. I just married into the family. So which one brought you here?"

"Cosmo" she answered. It wasn't a lie as such, well maybe it just wasn't the whole truth. She didn't know if she could trust this woman.

Zandra stated, "Us girls have to stick together, come with me! I'd say we don't have much time." She entered a door on her left. Megan followed as if this was all a bad dream and she would wake up any second to find herself buried under shelves in the storeroom. What choice did she have? Megan was relieved that the woman with the baby seemed normal compared to all the other crap surrounding her right now.

"I'm Zandra by the way, and this is Iva." She said as she placed the baby on a change table and began to attend to the baby's nappy.

"Megan, my name's Megan." She stumbled over her own name. God, she hoped she woke up soon. She was starting to feel less than sane.

"Ok Megan, let's just say, I've been there, done that and have the baby and T-shirt to prove it," Zandra confided, remembering her own journey.

"What my mother-in-law neglects to mention is that as humans, we have free will and she can't take that away. What you need to do is decide what you want."

Megan needed time to think and she needed space to do that. "I need to get out of here, but I don't know how? It's like a revolving door."

Zandra finished changing Iva's nappy, placed her in the crib, flicked the switch on the musical wind chimes over the cot and smiled. Her daughter was one of the most precious things in her life and she wouldn't change for anything.

Zandra fished her mobile out of her pocket, pressed a couple of buttons, and placed the phone on speaker.

"Hey, my gorgeous girl! How you doing?

How's my beautiful goddaughter?" The voice on the loud speaker sounded over-excited to be hearing from Zandra.

"Good and good. Look JT, I need a favour?" Zandra admitted.

JT laughed, "You know me, I'm your go-to girl. What do need?"

Zandra conspired with JT with Megan listening in. Megan felt a pang of jealousy. She'd never had a friendship like these women had. She'd always been a loner. Sure she had acquaintances but no one she could call on in a pinch. Feeling awkward, she glanced away not wanting Zandra to see her misted eyes. She ran her tongue against the roof of her mouth to stop them from leaking.

"Ok, so you can be here in about thirty-five for a pick up n' run. I'll check out a delivery address and have that sorted by the time you get here." Zandra disconnected the call and turned to Megan.

"Now all we need to do is get you showered and dressed and ready to go. While you're doing that, I'll take care of my side and get a hotel organized."

Zandra led the way to the bathroom. She stopped on the way to raid the closet for jeans and a shirt. "Can you live without underwear for a day till you get yourself sorted?"

Megan nodded, "Yeah I'll live." She gave a shaky smile, "Why are you doing all this? You don't even know me."

"Free will," Zandra laughed.

"What will Cosmo do when she finds out you helped me?" Megan asked, with a guilty feeling that she may have dropped Zandra in it when the goddess found out.

Zandra smiled, "Don't, I'm the mother of her grandchild and I've got Destiny on my side."

Forty minutes later with a kiss on the cheek and a hug from JT, Zandra waved Megan off, swapping cell phone numbers, and details of the hotel's address were passed on to JT.

She re-entered her home and headed for the library where her Destiny had been working hard at fulfilling his duties.

In this room he was blind, but he'd long ago memorized every curve, and angle of her body. The adrenalin coursed through her system making her ache for him. She closed the door and moved toward the desk.

Destiny rolled his chair back, allowing his wife to slide in front of him. He wrapped his arms around her, swiping everything from his desk. He shifted her ass on the edge as she ripped her shirt over her head and released her bra. He popped the button on her jeans as she leaned back to lift helping him to remove them. He raised her feet one at a time to free them from the denim then placed them on each armrest of his chair. He ran his hands up the inside of her legs, his thumbs separating her slick lips. He rolled his chair closer, spreading her wider before his head lowered to run his tongue along her weeping centre.

Destiny loved the way Zandra's body always responded so eagerly to his touch. The sounds she made when he pleasured her fed his own desire.

He licked circles around her swollen nub and he teased the sensitive nerves, as she squirmed in ecstasy. She was close to the edge as he worked her into a frenzy of need, then slid his thumb inside her pussy. With his palm facing up, he curled the tip, with just the right pressure on her spot, her orgasm gushed over his face and hand. Unable to hold himself in check any longer, he stood, lowered his sweats and placed the head of his engorged cock at her convulsing entry, with one hard stroke he buried himself deep. He felt for her legs and lifted them to his shoulders. Zandra's body collapsed. Her back on the desk, her hands raised over her head to take hold. Destiny leaned forward, his hands slapped flat on the desk top. Zandra's legs widened giving better access as Destiny began a slow deep pussy-drenching rhythm. God, she loved the way he filled her. There was nowhere she couldn't feel him. He was in her head, her heart and her soul. They were one. As Destiny grew harder still inside her walls, he increased the speed and power of his thrust. His thumb joined his ministrations with pressure on her clit. He drove her to her second explosive orgasm taking himself right along with her. His hot seed pulsing inside her twitching pussy. He collapsed over her, her legs fell heavy like dead weight, she was well loved by her man. He kissed her after he regained his breath and whispered against her lips, "I love you." She kissed the tip of his nose, "I love you too."

JT PULLED INTO THE CAR PARK OF THE HOTEL and turned in her seat. "Are you doing ok? You've been really quiet since I told you where we are." They had stopped at a branch of Megan's bank on the way and she had managed to withdraw some of her emergency money. Luckily they had her signature on computerized file. She had enough money to last out the week in her pocket for food, clothes and to get home. She prayed she still had a home to go to after the cyclone had passed.

"Yeah, I'm fine, thanks. I guess I'm just really exhausted, what with the cyclone, then being relocated." She kept tight lipped about most of it since she had no idea how much Zandra had said in regards to her home or family life.

"Well good luck and if you need anything give one of us a call," JT said as Megan opened the car door.

DESTRUCTION HAD LET MEGAN RUN. THAT had been some time ago now, not that he'd been counting.

He busied himself by checking the map, moving items slightly. He'd added a couple and taken some away. It was like an elaborate game of chess, except he had no opponent. The situation became boring very quickly.

He had planned to move the cyclone on the coast of Australia out to sea, but then for purely personal reasons, he moved it closer adding a little more intensity to it. If the cyclone wasn't there anymore it meant it would be safe for Megan to return home. He couldn't let that happen just yet. He wanted to get to know Megan. No, he needed to get to know her. Something bone deep in his soul knew she was his female. He simply needed to convince her of it too.

He snapped out of his thoughts, and went looking for her. His senses suddenly flaring, his gut turned in knots when he couldn't find her anywhere. Where the fuck was she?

CHAPTER 10

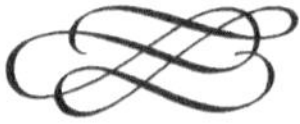

Megan stood at the window of her hotel room, the weather had turned bad. The cyclone had moved closer to the coast and was now rated at level five. All roads in and out had been closed off.

She yawned so hard her jaw popped. She rubbed her arms to warm the bone-deep chill of exhaustion away. She won't be going anywhere until it eased up outside.

She needed to let Zandra know about Troy. She felt like she had betrayed the woman's trust by omission. She texted the number in her pocket quickly to relieve her guilt.

· · ·

Hi Zandra,

I'm sorry I didn't tell you sooner, but I ran from Troy. He may be looking for me.
Thank you for all your help. - Megan

She pressed send. A short while later the phone chirped as she was about to climb into bed. She picked up the jeans from the chair and dug into the pocket. She flipped it open, and read the screen.

Hi Megan

Sorry was busy,
Troy, Huh? Could have done with a heads up on that one. Storm front headed our way. Take care.
Z

"I'm gonna wake up and find this was all a bad dream, I just bumped my head on something in the storeroom." She tried to convince herself as she pulled back the sheets. She slid in thinking there's nothing like fresh sheets when you're really tired.

She was out cold within seconds of her head hitting the pillow.

She woke to the feel of her nipples so hard they ached, her pussy throbbing and the remnants of a very wet dream.

She lifted her hands to cup her breasts, then trapped their hard cherries between her thumb and forefinger, and rolled them. The sensation was so sweet it caused her back to arch off the bed. She scissored her legs but it did nothing to ease the pulse in her pussy. She slid her right hand down her stomach, to her slit. She pressed her fingers between her outer lips. She was shocked at how wet she was. She probed her entrance with just the tips of her fingers, then moved them up along the smooth, sensitive skin between her pussy and clit. She lowered her other hand to hold her lips up and back to expose the head of her nub. Again, she followed the same pattern with the barest of touch on her clit. It reminded her of Troy's tongue, and with that thought engraved in her mind she was lost. She needed to cum so bad her entire body trembled. In her head, she could picture his eyes lifting to meet hers, silently demanding her to cum for him. She had never pleasured herself with this much intensity, as her orgasm roared to life in full force. It was good but nowhere near as good as when Troy touched her. She'd never put a face to her fantasy. She exploded with ecstasy.

He was her dragon. Now that he'd touched her, she would crave him like chocolate. Saddened, she rolled over and snagged the pillow next to her. She fell asleep cuddled up to it, with the memory of what it was like to wake in the arms of Destruction.

DESTRUCTION SEARCHED HIS REALM, HIS mood had become dangerous, and he'd been negligent in locking his door again. He knew it was the only way she could have left.

He had to find her. If she managed to persuade one of his siblings to help her to go home, she could already be dead. The taste in his mouth turned sour at the thought, but with his emotions so volatile, he didn't dare go near his library.

He could put the call out to his brother Destiny, but he only knew Megan's first name.

He was struggling to figure out a way to find her, when the air shifted behind him. He spun around swiftly to find his mother and she did not look happy.

"What is your distress, my son? Your emotions are all over the place and the human world is starting to suffer as a result. You need to calm yourself," she stated.

"Mother, what are you playing at? Where is Megan?" His emotions flared.

"Don't take that tone with me, my son. I wasn't the one to that let her run out of here," she chastised.

"Even if I knew where to start looking, how am I supposed to go after her when everything I touch is destroyed?" He was growing more and more frustrated with the whole situation.

"I will offer you the same deal I offered your brother Destiny. You will need to venture to the human realm. I believe Destiny may be able to guide you there. The moment you enter the human realm time will be of the essence. I will allow you three days to find her and bring her home of her own free will. If she does not come of her own free will, then you will return alone and that will be the end of it. Do you understand my conditions?"

"Yes, but I still won't be able to touch anything in the human realm without leaving destruction in my path." He wouldn't risk injury to Megan or her world no matter how much he wanted her.

"I'll gift you with the ability to walk in her world. You will still be strong and it will be the strength of a human. However, this arrangement must not be spoken of to anyone, including Megan." There was still one catch she'd neglected to mention.

"Do you agree to my terms and condition?" She waited, knowing the answer but needing to hear it.

"Yes, and thank you mother." He made a

move to pack a bag. He was leaving straight away.

"You will need this," she said. As she raised her hand, an hour glass sat in her palm. "The sand will start to shift the moment you walk through that door." She pointed to the door at the end of the hall.

CHAPTER 11

Destruction walked through the door at the end of the hall, closing it behind him and locking it.

He approached his brother Destiny's door. Testing his mother's promise of human strength, he lifted his hand, formed a fist, and knocked. His eyebrows lifted when the door didn't splinter from its hinges.

He smiled to himself and knocked again with more urgency, until he heard the lock shift and the door crack open a few scant inches.

Zandra stepped back out of the way, a

look of fear on her face, she said, "I was wondering when you would show up?"

"Is Destiny around? I need to speak with him. It's urgent." His eyes were looking at the door and its frame in wonder.

"He's with Iva. I'll get him for you." Zandra started down the hall to where Destiny was playing with his daughter.

She startled when she noticed that Destruction had followed. She was even more shocked when she realized there was no indication that he hadn't left any damage in his wake.

"Baby, your brother is here and you really need to see him." Her eyes were as wide as saucers.

Destiny stood from where he had been helping Iva feed shapes into a ball. He lifted his daughter to pass her to her mother. He looked past his wife to see Troy as he leaned against the door jam. Was he missing something? His brother had a duffle bag over his shoulder, like he was going somewhere.

"Troy, what's going on?" he asked, with a look of concern shadowing his face.

"I need your help. I need to find my female." He wasn't sure how Destiny was supposed to do that exactly.

"Do you know her name?" Destiny thought he'd start with her journal.

"Yes and no, her first name is Megan, but that's all I've got." Things were not moving fast enough for his liking.

Zandra cleared her throat behind Destiny. She was at odds with herself. She hadn't had time to mention anything about her afternoon escapade. Would he be ticked off at what she had done and that she had not told him. He might think she was keeping secrets.

All her thoughts kept coming back full circle. There was something going on with Destruction and her gut was telling her she needed to dog her girl Megan out. She crossed her fingers behind her back and hoped for the best, for everyone.

She cleared her throat again to try and find her voice. It came out barely louder than a whisper. "I know where Megan is."

Both men turned to stare at Zandra, her cheeks flamed. She suddenly felt like she was back in high school standing in the principal's office.

In unison, the brothers asked, "What?"

With a shaky breath and repeated herself, "I know where Megan is." She regained control over her inner woman and added, "To make a long story short, I helped a sister out. She said she needed space and time to figure things out, so I had JT pick her up and take her to a hotel."

Destiny did not look happy about this new development, making a mental note that he would spank her ass later.

"Zandra, I need to be with her. You hold the only way I have of finding her. Will you help a brother out?" he asked.

She figured, 'what the hey!' "I'll write the address down for you," She was about to get a pen and paper when it crossed her mind that there might be a quicker way. "If I show you on a GPS, can you do that vanish thing?"

Destruction liked the way Zandra thought, "I sure can, just point me in the right direction."

Zandra quickly entered the info into her

phone and brought up the details. Passing the phone to Destruction, he memorized its location.

Zandra explained that the room was booked under her name not Megan's.

Destruction handed the phone back to Zandra and gave her a sly smile, "Thanks, wish me luck?"

He turned to his brother, clapped him on the back, and vanished.

CHAPTER 12

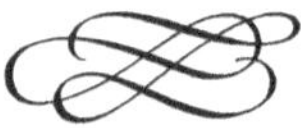

Destruction looked around the hotel lobby before he took solid form in a secluded corner.

A runaway child who was trying to evade capture was frozen in his tracks. He winked at the small boy as he moved passed him. The kid quickly turned back to the shelter of his parents. He didn't worry about what the kid had seen; nobody would believe him anyway.

He approached the service desk and waited. As the young woman behind the counter finished with another couple, he took a complimentary piece of paper and a pen from the counter-top and scribbled

'Gotcha' and a smiley face. Folded the note and waited.

The young woman gave him a sickly sweet smile as she moved toward him which left him feeling dirty. "How can I help you sir?" she said flirtatiously.

"Can I leave a message for Zandra Chancellor? She might be listed as Wilson." He wasn't sure which last name had been used.

"Definitely sir, I'll just get you a receipt for that." She looked up the room number and deposited the note in the corresponding pigeon hole. She turned back to him and wrote something on the back of the hotel card and passed it to him.

He was more focused on the number above the box the note now resided in, room one thirty four. He smiled to himself. As he took the card, the woman behind the counter winked at him. As he walked away, he flipped the card over in his fingers. 'Are you fucking serious?' The counter clerk's name and phone number were on the back. He tossed it in the trash before walking out the front door, not giving a shit if she took offense and removed his note. He had all the info he needed. He studied the map of the hotel he had taken from counter. It listed the room numbers by floors.

He vanished. The first of the eleventh floor balconies he landed on had an old couple inside. The second one was empty, the lights were off and there was no movement. Third time was the charm; he found his woman naked, tangled in sheets. As his emotions flared, lightening lit up the sky.

MEGAN OPENED HER EYES IN FEAR; SHE HAD always disliked thunder storms. She lifted her head. She must have been dreaming. She blinked quickly to clear her sleep-glazed eyes. She could have sworn she saw Troy outside her glass sliding door within the flash of lightening.

Lightning and thunder always made her feel uneasy. If the cyclone up the coast was causing messy weather here, she could only imagine what her home town was being hounded like. She would be lucky to have a home to go back to.

She rolled over to climb out of bed. Maybe a shower would clear her thoughts and ease her nerves till the worst of the storm passed. Another crash of lightning and thunder made her jump. She screamed as strong arms wrapped around her. "Shhh, I've got you, Shhh." She fought the strong arms, as her brain registered the soft command in Troy's voice.

Her mother's old saying was playing in the back of her mind like a recorded message. 'May lightning strike me dead on the spot if I'm lying' Fuck, she couldn't lie even to herself, she was glad he was here. She could slap her mother for instilling a cosmic fear of storms in her so strongly it was now a phobia. Astra-fucking-phobia. She had tried to overcome it but nothing worked and now fear was coursing through her system at lightning speed.

She pushed away from Troy, "I'm gonna be sick," she said as she raced to the bathroom.

Troy followed close behind. He held her hair back from her face as she started to heave. After she emptied her stomach's contents, she stood, turned, flipped the lid shut on the toilet, and sat down. She kept repeating in her mind, 'I'm safe, it can't get me, and I'm inside.' It still didn't stop the cold sweats and the trembles wracking her body.

Troy quickly took the wash cloth off the counter along with the complimentary bottles of shampoo, conditioner and body wash. He placed them on the shelf in the shower and started to strip. His female was in a terrified state and he needed to get things under his control. He turned on the shower. He helped her to stand and steered her to the basin. He handed her a toothbrush loaded with paste turning on the faucet. She was pale, her eyes glazed with tears of fear that tore at his heart.

While she mechanically cleaned her teeth, he caged her from behind with his naked body. He lowered his head to her shoulder and again said, "Shhh, I've got you. You're safe with me."

At the contact of his soft lips on her bare-skinned shoulder, she let lose a sob.

She leant, over spat out the froth filling her mouth, and rinsed.

As she stood back up, her eyes met his. This was way too embarrassingly personal. He was seeing her at her weakest. Through the frosted window she saw the bright flash of another strike of light. Her heart pounded harder and faster in her chest.

He turned her in his arms, lowered his lips to her ears, and with a low softly command he whispered, "Focus on me, nothing else, I've got you." His arms surrounded her waist.

He lifted her gently and moved to the shower. He stepped them both inside. After her feet were back on solid tiles, he closed the door. He removed the shower head from the wall, tilted her chin up and soaked her hair. Troy's gentleness and comfort was working deeper than the shampoo on her scalp and in her curls. She closed her eyes to savour the sensations that were teasing her body. He washed her hair twice and conditioned it, each time removing the shower head for the purpose of a thorough rinse.

She had never felt cherished before. The

icy barriers around her heart were starting to melt.

He grabbed the wash cloth, rinsed it and softly wiped her face. Taking the body wash next, he combined the two to form a lather. He teased her neck, watching the suds mix with water and run down over her tightly-budded nipples. She moaned as she lost all concept of time and space. He lifted one arm at a time, working in circles to her fingertips. He turned her and placed her palms flat on the tile wall. "Stay." His command was husky with desire.

He worshipped her body with the lather. It made his cock fill with want. But he focused his attention on his female's needs.

He again turned her submissive body to rest her shoulders against the tiles as he manipulated the cloth over her sensitized nipples. The water spray chased the suds away as he lowered his head to lick at the tips. She gasped, her pussy gushed with a contraction. The empty ache in her inner walls almost painful. "Am I hurting you?" he asked with concern.

"No, um, yes," she replied breathlessly. "I ache."

He tossed the cloth on the shelf, rinsed his hand of soap, then cupped her breasts in both hands. He ran his thumbs over their puckered buds before taking them one at a time licking and sucking them. As he toyed with her need, he slid his hand down between their bodies, lightly brushing his knuckles over the red stubble-covered lips. Her fingernails dug into his shoulders leaving crescent moons. If his hard body didn't have her wedged against the wall her legs would have given way. He lifted his head to take possession of her mouth. As a clap of thunder and lightning fought to take back her attention, his fingers entered her slick channel. His tongue matching his fingers' invasion. "Mmmm," she moaned, becoming almost frenzied with her body's demand to be taken.

His hands took purchase of her plump ass as he lifted her. His cock slid between her folds, coating it in her slick juices as it nudged over her clit. He angled his hips as she locked her ankles behind him plunging deep, his mouth captured her strangled moan. He stilled, with the head of his cock against her cervix, giving her time to adjust to his size.

He slowly withdrew till just his crown was surrounded by her swollen lips. He savoured the feel of her muscles around him, as they tried to suck him back into their depths. She squirmed against him in need. Unable to resist the temptation any longer, he began to ride her hard and deep. Long strokes became quicker as he felt the tingle in the base of his spine. His thumb moved to where their bodies met, drawing her slippery essence up to tease her clit. They both fell over the edge with an explosion of lightning and thunder, drowning out the chorus of their climax.

CHAPTER 13

Destruction's emotions were all over the place. His head unable to focus on anything but the woman in his arms.

They were standing in front of the closed glass door, Megan in the white hotel bathrobe and him with a towel anchored around his waist.

Her back was to his chest as they watched the storm seething on the other side. She still jumped when the lightning struck in the distance, but in his arms she was no longer in a state of panic.

He had broken through more than just the barriers around her heart. She felt with him by her side, she could take on the world. Even her phobia.

"What are you doing here?" she asked.

"I want to get to know you, to see if there might be something between us worth fighting for," he answered.

"Well I don't know about you, but I'm hungry. I might be ok standing here watching the storm with you but there's no way I'm going out in it. There's two choices, we can go downstairs to the restaurant or we can order room service. I'm leaning towards room service. How about you?" she asked as her stomach growled.

"Room service sounds great," figuring it would give them more time together without any possible interruptions.

Destruction went to his bag, unzipped it and was reminded by what little time he had. Even laid on its side, the damn hour glass sand still managed to drain away.

His thoughts were distracted by the hour glass as he pulled free a pair of sweats and tugged them on. The storm outside increased in intensity. The sound of the rain was so loud it was near impossible to hear room service knock at the door.

Troy opened the door and stepped back out of the way. The service attendant wheeled in a cart with a number of silver domes, an ice bucket and a couple of glasses. There was a single stem red rose in the centre. The smells surrounding the cart were divine.

"If there's nothing else sir, you can leave the cart outside the door when you're done. Enjoy." The man excused himself closing and locking the door as he left.

Destruction stood there staring at the cart, not exactly sure what to do now. He'd hadn't seen anything like this in centuries. Not since before his twenty-first cycle.

Megan came up beside him and started to lift the silver domes. She handed him an empty plate. "I wasn't sure what you would like so I ordered a little of everything." She smiled and started to load up her own plate.

They sat next to each other at the dining table and ate quietly, sampling a little of everything. Damn, this was the best thing she'd ever eaten. The steak cooked to perfection, the salad crisp, and Troy seemed to be enjoying his just as much as she was. They hadn't spoken much through dinner, just smiles and glances at each other. Like they had a secret that nobody knew about except them.

She leaned back against her chair and sat her hands on her bloated belly. Destruction watched every mouthful pass her lips; he liked to see his female satisfied.

His eyes dipped to where her hands rested. He wondered if one day she would grow full and round with his child. God he hoped so, more than anything, he hoped so. His stomach full, he pushed his plate away. They sipped the wine while watching each other.

"What do we do now?" Megan asked.

"I don't know. I've never had a holiday. I have no idea what you would do for kicks," he said with a wink.

"Well, we could watch a movie?" she said as she cleared the table, loading the empty plates back on the cart. She moved the desert to the bar fridge for later.

She was starting to feel a sense of comfort being around Troy, the man. She didn't want to think about the immortal side of him, not now, not yet.

As a man he was her ideal, not that she'd spent that much time with him. They sat cuddled up together on the couch as she flicked on the big screen TV to pick a movie. Reality struck hard and fast.

The news headlines were proclaiming a national disaster along the coast. Houses had been flattened, crops ruined. They were forecasting flash floods in places that had been already stricken with drought. With tears running down her cheeks, she stood. Suddenly she needed distance. The movie forgotten, she continued to watch the news. Things were not only happening in her own part of the world. There seemed to be a whole lot of crazy tearing up the globe.

She had so many questions running through her head, they were all jumbled up and confusing.

Every time she tried to get answers, he would distract her by doing things to her body that disintegrated all logical thought.

Destruction could feel a physical chill in the room as the images on the screen showed the devastation and destruction. The shame of his duties weighed heavy on his soul. He couldn't look at Megan any longer. The tears in her eyes, her rigid stance, were ripping his heart out. He needed to leave. How could he expect her to want to be with him when he would only destroy her in the end? He stood and ventured to the bedroom. He packed up his bag, threw it over his shoulder, and returned to where Megan's attention was still transfixed on the screen.

Standing in front of her, he leaned down, brushed his lips over hers and whispered, "I love you." Then vanished.

CHAPTER 14

Megan lifted her hand to her lips. The tears she had shed for the scenes on TV were outweighed by tears she now cried for herself and the man who loved her.

Her legs gave way and she crumpled into a shaking heap of sobs. She thought she knew what it was like to lose the man she loved when she had lost Shaun. This however, was so much worse. This was devastating. She felt like her heart had been torn from her chest, a physical ache carved into her body to replace it.

She felt lost, like she no longer belonged anywhere. She couldn't go home even if she wanted to, but she didn't want to be here anymore either, not with all the memories Troy had created in such a short time here in this hotel room. She couldn't leave though. The storm was still threatening anyone stupid enough to go out in it. She was alone again, always alone.

DESTRUCTION RETURNED TO HIS REALM. HE threw his bag down and walked to the fridge. He opened it, looked at the bottles of beer inside, then slammed the door shut. He needed something stronger. He went to his bag on the floor, unzipped it and removed the hourglass. Gripping it tightly, he stormed to the library for the bottle of scotch.

Everything was fucked up. He'd had the chance at a future, a forever, and he had destroyed it. He felt ruined as he snatched the bottle, ripped off the cap and skulled a third of it, in three burning swallows. He dropped the hourglass to the floor, lifted his foot, and shattered it. He celebrated with another guzzle of scotch. Then turned and pitched the bottle at the nearest wall; glass exploded spewing the remnants.

Fuck he hated his existence. He wished there was some way Death could claim him. Take him away from it all.

The room swayed, his brother appeared at his side. He released a warrior's roar and with fists raised, he took aim.

Death side-stepped Troy's aggression. "What the fuck, man!"

"Argh!" Destruction again lunged at his brother. He vaporized and reappeared on the other side of the room. This time, Destruction picked up a chair and hurled it at his brother.

That was it. Death had had enough. Suddenly, he stood in front of Destruction pushing him back. He didn't care if this got messy. It wasn't his library after all and it had been too long since he'd had a good throw down. It was about time he unloaded some steam. If this was what his brother called him for, then he was about to bring it. Let the party begin.

As Destruction came at him, he threw his fist out, colliding with his jaw, following through with his elbow. He brought his elbow back into Destruction's solar plexus.

Destruction grabbed Death in a choke hold, one arm around his neck. Death's quick reaction had spun him free before Destruction could lock his arms together. The battle seemed to go on forever, with well-aimed knees, fists, elbows and kicks. They were evenly matched and knew they couldn't do any real physical damage to one another. But when it came down to it, it was all about ego, the bragging rights.

Finally, Destruction yelled, "GET OUT." Death was physically rejected from Destruction's realm as if he'd been tossed out, with the door hitting him in the ass on the way.

DEATH LANDED BACK IN HIS REALM, STILL confused about what his brother had called him for.

"Fuck you too, Asshole!" He said to no one. He was tired of this shit.

With his clothes ripped, he walked into

his room, grabbed a fresh set of leathers and a black muscle shirt. He threw them on the bed, removed his torn gear, and made his way to the shower.

Like he needed this crap. What made his family think his life was any better than theirs?

The next thing was to find Vanessa. It would be the last time she ran. He'd make sure of it.

MEGAN HAD CRIED HERSELF DRY BEFORE SHE was overtaken by exhaustion and felt herself falling asleep on the floor as she hugged a cushion to her hollow chest.

When she woke, she gathered herself up, turned to the bar fridge and indulged her broken heart by polishing off both deserts.

DESTRUCTION'S HEAD SWAYED SLIGHTLY, AS he sat on the edge of his bed. The rage within him had been doused by his brother challenge. He would have to explain himself to Death one day, just not right now. He hoped his brother would understand and cut him some slack.

He sprawled back on the bed, closed his eyes, and his torture began. He would never again close his eyes without seeing the image of his female. He would always crave the feel of her skin touching his. Always wanting to share her laughter, comfort her tears and pleasure her moans. He would end up going insane, from being deprived of that future.

CHAPTER 15

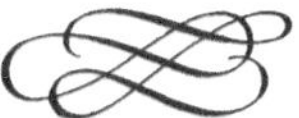

Megan was getting cabin fever from being locked up in the hotel room alone for so long. The TV was saying they could see no end in sight on the latest storm front travelling down the coast from up north.

It showed scenes of the beaches being eaten away, the waterfront a seething sea of foam.

The limited coverage of her home town showed houses flattened, trees uprooted and cars resting on their sides. Like they had been playing smash ups. Roads in were still closed due to flooding. Fuck it, she really wanted to get home, but she wanted see

Troy more than finding out if she even had a place to go home to.

It must have been the sugar rush that influenced her brain processor. There was a little voice telling her she was woman time to roar; put your big girl pants on, we're taking a road trip.

She packed up what little stuff she had, picked up the cell phone and made a quick call. While she waited, she put her shoes on. Shortly after, her phone beeped and she headed for the door. She was nervous as hell being outside, but there was no turning back now, the decision had been made.

DEATH FACED OFF AGAINST HIS MOTHER. "Now is not a good time, mother. Can we do this later?" He was thinking maybe the twelfth of never sounded real good for him. He wanted to start looking for Vanessa before she had too much of a head start.

Cosmo dug her heals in, "No. You know this is inevitable. You have to, it is time. I'm not going to stand here and argue about this."

Death suddenly saw his mother in a new light. She gave the humans free will, but refused to offer it to him. "Fine, I'll do it. Not like I ever have a choice." He closed his eyes, thinking of Vanessa and vanished.

DESTRUCTION WOKE IN A FOUL MOOD AFTER a restless night filled with dreams about Megan. As one dream had ended another began. He tossed and turned and wrestled in torture in a bed that still smelled of her.

He showered, dismissing the raging hard on for a woman he could no longer have. He continued to ignore it when he got dressed. Maybe if he kept ignoring it, it would eventually go the fuck away.

He went about his mundane duties, creating an earthquake in California, aggravating a volcano in Indonesia, a snow storm in Japan. He kept himself busy avoiding the cyclone. It was about time it fizzled out, but to kill the cyclone would be the definite end of him and Megan. He wasn't ready to face those facts so soon. He knew he had to, but he also knew that Megan would come to hate him once she returned home and saw the carnage on such a large scale. It was bad and it made it personal.

He couldn't do personal at the moment. If he could, he would be going after what he really wanted, fuck the world in his selfishness. So again, he deflected his attention from Megan's area on the map.

His thoughts were too dark at the moment. The power surging within him was lethal. He left the library and went to the kitchen even though food was the last thing on his mind.

ZANDRA PACED BACK AND FORTH. SHE HAD taken the phone call about an hour ago.

She needed to explain things to Destiny. She promised him she wouldn't keep anything from him ever again.

Although the punishment Destiny had implemented to prove his point might be worth revisiting, it was probably a little too soon to push those boundaries.

Her ass cheeks warmed at the memory of Destiny laying her over his lap, and lowering his hand in a firm slap. "Don't", slap, "Ever", slap, "Do", slap, "It again." The muscles in her bottom clenched at how unbelievably hot it had been. He teased her wet pussy, not allowing her to cum until she made the promise.

She stopped pacing outside the library door to check on Iva who was still sleeping soundly. As she returned, she took a deep steadying breath, and reached him out for the door knob. The door swung open. Destiny stalked her until her back hit the wall and then he pounced. His mouth crashed down on hers, in a snap he released her mouth, and spun her to face the wall trapping both hands between just one of his. He leaned in close to her ear and in a voice harshened by passion he asked, "If I didn't know any better, my beautiful wife, I'd think you were trying to hide something from me?" He smiled at the remembrance of spanking that curved ass, how wet she had become, and so quickly. He tilted his pelvis to wedge his hardening cock against her crevice-divided cheeks. The tip of his tongue tasted her lobe, his lips encasing it to suck seductively as if to mimic what he planned to do to her once he rid her of her clothes.

Zandra moaned, pushing her ass back at him, grinding her hips, as her hot pussy gushed in excitement.

His free hand slid under her shirt to tease her nipple through its lace casing. Their heavy breathing almost loud enough to drown out the sound of a car pulling up outside.

He nipped Zandra's ear, as she groaned in sexual frustration. "We will finish this later. We have company," he said.

JT STOPPED THE CAR AS CLOSE TO THE FRONT door as the driveway would allow. "You ready?" She asked. Megan gave a nod. She hoped it was convincing, she wasn't feeling as confident now that she was here.

They opened the car doors simultaneously and made a run for it. A crash of thunder and a flash of lightening and Megan froze. A second spark of lightening and rumble caused her to jump moments later, eliciting a screech.

JT looked over her shoulder as she reached the shelter of the front porch to see Megan, as white as a ghost, at a standstill.

She turned back and took her by the hand, "Close your eyes, I'll take the lead. You just follow, one foot in front the other."

Megan did as she was told, cursing herself for lying about being ready for this. She had to be ready for this, she didn't have a choice, she couldn't stay in that hotel room another minute. But a lie was a lie; would she ever be ready for this?

JT guided her to the front door, knocked and waited for Zandra to open it.

DESTINY HEARD THE POUNDING FIST AT THE front door. He knew that impatient knock. He released his hold on his wife and quickly moved to open it. Just as he thought, JT stood there with a woman by her side. Both were drenched. "This better be good JT. Your timing sucks."

"Do you think I go out of my way to mess with you and your mojo?" JT didn't like being reminded she still hadn't found her mizz right. "Why don't you help a sister out and fix me up? Seeing as you hold all the answers in that department?"

"JT, you know very well that's not how things work, and even if I could find your journal, there's no guarantee." Destiny had, for Zandra's sake looked in his library but had never been able to locate her friend's journal.

Destiny stepped back out of the way so JT and Megan could enter. "'Bout time, you big oaf. I thought you were going to leave us out there to freeze." She pushed past Destiny to reach her friend, "You didn't tell him did you?" she asked with a cheeky grin, shaking her head.

"No. I was about to but he distracted me." Zandra blushed.

"You're so bad," JT laughed wickedly.

Megan stood in the doorway dripping all over the mat. She knew she was staring, but couldn't help herself.

Destiny extended his hand as he introduced himself, "I'm Destiny, Zandra's husband."

"Megan, Megan Delaney," she said, still staring. The resemblance between this man and the man she was in love with was obvious. "Oh My God! You're Troy's brother?"

CHAPTER 16

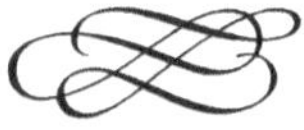

Megan, Zandra and JT converged in the bedroom. They needed time to talk girl stuff.

JT grabbed her overnight bag out of the boot of her car, and Megan borrowed some clothes from Zandra.

If she was going to do this right, she had to get a move on before she wimped out and left with her tail between her legs.

She asked Zandra if she had any scotch. She needed a nip of Dutch courage to put one foot in front of the other.

She threw the shot back like a pro, then asked JT and Zandra to wish her luck. She stepped it out like she was a mission, her hand paused on the door knob at the end of the hall. She took a calming breath, opened the door and stepped through to take control of her future.

DESTRUCTION HAD GIVEN UP ON HIS DUTIES for the day. He lay in bed tossing and turning unable to let sleep take him.

He sat up, rifled through the drawer of the bedside table and his hand found his brothers sand pouch. He probably shouldn't use the stuff after last time, but he figured 'Fuck It.' If this was all he had, he'd take it.

He dipped his thumb into the sand and lifted it to his forehead then sat the bag beside the lamp. He laid back down and closed his eyes.

ZANDRA TOLD MEGAN TO TAKE THE THIRD door to the left. She found the door knob, and begged the universe to find it unlocked. Holding her breath, she turned the knob.

The door opened quietly. She sent up a silent thank you.

She stole into Troy's realm as stealthily as a cat burglar. She took her shoes off to avoid making any undue noise. She listened intently for any signs of Troy indicating where he might be. She heard nothing. Carefully, she tiptoed to the library. Once inside, she closed the door and turned on the light. Observing the map she looked to pinpoint the place where she used to live. It only took her a minute. She moved the amulet closest to that area. Out in the middle of the ocean. Satisfied that the cyclone threat had been diverted, she made her way back to the door. Flicking the light off as she exited the library.

DESTRUCTION WAS DREAMING OF HIS beautiful female, she was on her back, legs wide open to him.

He was buried in her honey pot, feasting on her succulent flesh. "Tell me you want me," he commanded. He teased her, waiting to hear her beg for him to take her.

MEGAN HEARD A MOAN COME FROM THE direction of Troy's bedroom. Okay, she thought, never having done anything like this before, she figured, 'Here goes nothing.'

She silently entered the darkened bedroom and stood at foot of the bed.

She watched the rise and fall of Troy's naked chest. Wanting to see more of her man, she snagged the sheet, sliding it carefully down his body. God he was magnificent, all strong lines and solid muscle.

The sheet pooled at her feet, she removed her clothes, and added them to the pile of material on the floor.

Her body was humming with excitement as she carefully climbed up onto the bed resisting the urge to touch him prematurely. She felt like a tigress stalking its prey. She hovered over his cock. Taking one last look at his handsome face, she licked her lips in anticipation. She flattened her tongue and started at the base, trailing it to the crown. His hardness jerked in response, his lips parted on a throaty groan. Embrazened, she again lowered her mouth, her tongue ran around the rim of the mushroom-shaped head, as if licking an ice cream while it melted. It twitched against her tongue. She puckered her lips and eased him into her mouth inch by inch. Once her mouth encased him, she took hold of the base to better guide him. He subconsciously bent one knee, opening up to her. She boldly spread her legs apart, her wickedness had rendered her wet and thrumming. Her free hand worked between her own legs, her clit was swollen with lust, throbbing. Her wet pussy was aching. She rolled her tongue around the head before sucking the length of it to the back of her throat. All the while, her fingers dipped into her love duct. The base of her palm applying the perfect pressure to her nub. She was close but it wasn't enough.

Destruction was lost amidst the most exquisite dream he'd ever had. He lowered his hand down his body, his cock craved release.

His hand became interwoven in silken strands. He knew the feel of Megan's soft red curls.

As his hold on sleep faltered, his dream wavered. He surfaced lucid, his fingertips came in contact with soft lips, and he could feel where his cock slid inside Megan's mouth.

"Megan?" he croaked, questioning his own sanity.

Megan resumed her sucking motion, unable to speak, she 'mmmmm'ed.' The vibrations had his back arching, wanting to follow the sound all the way down her throat.

The tingle started in the base of his spine, his balls tightened. Without warning he was spending his seed in Megan's mouth.

Megan swallowed every drop like she was savouring salted caramel. Unashamed, she worked towards her own release, frenzied by the power she had over his body.

The ability to rule it, to take control, had her shaking in rapture. Hot bliss covered her fingers as she exploded seeing stars. She lifted her head from his softening prick, "Argh!" She screamed praise, to herself, to her man, to anyone within hearing distance. She giggled to herself. Who would have thought she was a screamer.

She gathered her spent body and climbed up over Troy. She settled down on top of him. She kissed his chest and sighed.

He wrapped his arms around the woman he loved, would always love. "Megan?" His voice apprehensive.

"Mmmm?" She was tired, she just needed to rest a minute.

The sound of her response had him hardening quickly. It's the noise she had used to send him over the edge.

"What are you doing here?" he asked, pensively.

Megan's words came out on a yawn, "I wanted to get to know you better." She smiled to herself, his words given back to him all wrapped up in after sex glow.

Unable to resist, he rolled them both.

His stamina regained, he slid in between her slippery lips. Without pause he rammed home, that's what his woman was to him.... Home. He didn't have gentle or nice in him right now, so he fucked her, hard and fast. No this was not just a fuck, this was him claiming his mate and not taking no for an answer.

"Tell me Megan, why did you come here?" He would not let her cum until she gave him the answer he wanted. He needed to hear it with every fibre of his being.

"I.... wanted to get.... To know you better." She said, her head swaying back and forth on the pillow.

"Not good enough Megan," he demanded. He slid out of her body. She whimpered.

He briskly rolled her over, lifted her to her knees, spreading his to the outside. He placed a hand in between her shoulders pressing, silently instructing her to lower her swaying breasts to the mattress. He entered her in one forceful stroke.

Her hands were beside her turned head, curled into the sheets as she felt him to the hilt. She was filled to the brim, nowhere left for him to go, and she loved it. She loved him.

Without moving, he asked again, "Why Megan? Why are you here?"

She couldn't lie to herself any longer, she knew the truth. "Because I love you!" She yelled in exasperation. She couldn't take any more delays. She needed him, soul deep, and the last of her walls around her heart crashed down.

He heard her words, unleashing something inside him. If she was not already carrying the consequences of his love for her, she would be by the time he was done. Even if it destroyed them both.

He slid out to the tip, "Say it again," he demanded, as he surged home.

She moaned, "I love you... Argh! Troy, don't stop please, God yes! Like that." She was pushing back hard to meet his every stroke.

He leaned over her, his chest to her back. He bit her shoulder, making her muscles clench tighter around him. He eased her body up, sitting back on his knees skin to skin. He kissed her neck up to her ear, nipped the lobe and growled, "Touch yourself while I'm inside you." Her hips swayed, lifting and lowering onto his juice slickened organ. He lowered her back down to the mattress, spread her legs wider and rode hard to the finish.

She gushed with the detonation of her orgasm, "That's it baby, cum for me, cum all over my cock." His dirty talk had her second orgasm overriding the first. Her pussy contracting furiously keeping him anchored in a tight fist of molten lava as his seed exploded like a volcano. He collapsed to the bed, taking her with him, still buried deep. His life was in her hands.

CHAPTER 17

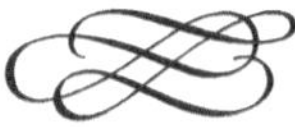

Troy woke Megan several times through the night, taking her on various journeys of pleasure. He would never get enough of her.

In the morning, she sat on a stool in the kitchen having coffee while Troy cooked breakfast. The man was seriously talented. She was enjoying the view when the air between them shimmered. Instantly, Cosmo appeared and was standing in front of her.

Troy turned at the intrusion, "Mother?"

She raised her hand to silence him.

"I realize that this is not good timing on my part, but this can't wait. Megan, I need to have a word with you, in private," Cosmo stated. It was not a request.

After everything Megan had been through, she did not want to go toe to toe with Cosmo, but she would if the situation called for it.

Megan braced the kitchen bench and stood.

"Destruction, I will speak with you shortly after I've heard what Megan has to say." Cosmo dismissed her son for the moment. Without a word, Cosmo walked towards the library. Megan looked at Troy with worry in her eyes but followed anyway.

What did the goddess want? Megan was nervous as she entered the library. As she cleared the entrance, Cosmo closed the door behind them.

"Take a seat dear," Cosmo said pointing to the couch. She herself choosing to stand, choosing not to sit, Megan recognized the motion as a stand-over technique. Her father used to use it to obtain the upper hand when displaying authority. It never worked for her father, but it never stopped him from trying. She gave an inner smirk. 'Let's see what you got, Cosmo,' she thought. She guessed after last night, she was feeling pretty damn ballsy and to top it off, she hated the word dear. She was not her mother or aging aunt, so she found it patronizing.

"Well, I suppose now that the cyclone has been diverted away from your home, it's safe to take you back?" Cosmo said glancing at the map behind her. She gave Megan a knowing look. Megan knew that she was busted on that one, but what life did she really have to go back to? Her parents were dead, and if she left Troy's realm, would she ever see him again?

"What if I don't want to go back? What if I want to stay here?" She needed to know that the option, that the choice was hers.

Cosmo smiled conspiringly, "Why would you want to stay?"

She looked at her hands in her lap, before raising her eyes and with conviction she replied, "I'm in love with Troy."

"Within the count of a few days, you claim to have fallen in love with my son,

Destruction? Are you in love with the man Troy, or my son, the God of Destruction?"

Megan stood from where she had been sitting, "Are they not one in the same?" Megan had already had time to think about this long and hard after Troy kissed her and left the hotel room that night. The resolution she came to was that she couldn't love one without loving the other. It was a package deal.

"Do you not fear my son? What if he destroys you?" Cosmo had already heard all she needed to hear, but Megan's way of thinking intrigued her.

"Look, I could go back, I also could step in front of a bus, and die tomorrow. What will be, will be. If I have one day with Troy or a hundred days, I will still love him. I will rest in peace knowing that I had whatever time I could with him."

Cosmo smiled, "Thank you for having the insight to see past the man. I think I've heard all I need. Would you tell my son, I'll see him now?"

~

DESTRUCTION WAS GOING OUT OF HIS MIND. What was his mother doing? He had a good mind to go to the library and bust in on his mother. His protectiveness towards Megan kicked in and he couldn't stand there in the kitchen not knowing any longer. He stormed to the closed library door. As he reached for it, it opened.

Megan gave him a sarcastic smile, "Your turn."

As she went to pass him, he reached out to her draw her into his arms and kissed her like his life depended on it. He kissed her thoroughly until he heard his mother cough, impatiently.

CHAPTER 18

Megan watched as Troy closed the library door. She couldn't walk away though. She crossed the wall and leaned back against it staring intently at closed door. As if she would miraculously develop X-ray vision and be able to see what was going down on the other side of it. No wait, she needed sonic hearing. That way she could hear what was being said. Who was she kidding? She wanted to bust through that door and defend her man, even if it was against the mighty powerful Cosmo. She slid down the wall, resting on her ass, she pulled her legs up and continued to stare. How long had he been in there already?

~

DESTRUCTION CLOSED THE DOOR, THEN turned to face his mother. "What's this all about?" he demanded.

Cosmo gave him a caustic smile, "You best not take that tone with me son, not if you want things to end favourably for you."

The puzzle pieces started to click together in Troy's mind. "You're not taking Megan away." he said defensively. He would never allow it.

"That all depends." Cosmo had already made her mind up. "If I do you won't be able to stop me, you realize?"

He silently glared at his mother, daring her to. He would destroy his mother's playthings, the human realm would cease to exist. She would have to exile him. Take away his power. A sudden thought crossed his mind. "If you take Megan from me, I will follow her. I will find a way to be with her, even if it means I can never touch her again." It wasn't a threat, it was a fact. He could not live without her. The hours he'd spent away from her after he left the hotel had been pure torture.

Cosmo looked at the sincerity in her son's eyes, "Would you be willing to become human?"

Destruction didn't hesitate, "Yes!"

Cosmo smiled, "That won't be necessary. Would you ask Megan to join us? I have a proposition for the both of you."

Destruction raced to the door, threw it open and saw the worried eyes of his female. He crossed to where she sat, giving her his hand, and he lifted her to her feet. He kissed her as she leaned into his arms. He felt like home at the end of a long day soothing her frayed nerves.

He kissed her softly, until Cosmo coughed, then released her to guide her back into the library.

"I have a proposition for the both of you. The decision must be unanimous, otherwise it won't happen. Do you both understand?"

In unison, they replied, "Yes."

Cosmo raised both hand to waist height,

palm up, she lowered her head. Within the blink of an eye, two journals and a small intricately carved box appeared to fill her hands.

"Megan, would you do anything within your power to stay with my son, whether it be here or in the human realm?"

Megan quickly responded, "Yes! I love him," confused by what was happening.

"Destruction, would you do anything in your power to stay with Megan, whether it be here in your home or in the human realm?" Cosmo directed her question to Destruction.

Troy's response mirrored Megan's, "Yes, I love her!"

"Destruction, come forward and acquire the box on top. Please present it to Megan as a sign of your eternal love." Troy did as he was instructed. He lifted the lid to see a ring, removing it from its seat. He turned to Megan.

"Megan, while ever you wear this ring, you will not age, you will not die, eternity is a long time. If you want forever with my son, then allow him to place it on your finger."

Megan raised a shaky hand, she was praying that this was not just a dream. She looked from Troy to Cosmo. Cosmo smiled and winked at her.

The ring slid onto her finger, a perfect fit. She looked down at it, then lifted her eyes to meet Troy's as everything started to get wavy. Fuck, she was crying like a big girl. Troy wiped away her tears then kissed her tenderly.

"Hmmm hmm," Cosmo interrupted. As they looked to where she stood, she informed them, "You are my son's destiny and he is yours." She handed them their journals. "A couple of small details before I go. I will bestow upon you the same gifts I have given Destiny and Zandra. Let me know if you wish to live as they do in the human realm. Think about the location and get back to me when you decide."

Megan overcome by gratitude, not really giving much thought to her actions, raced to Cosmo and hugged her.

Cosmo, unsure what do, placed a kiss on

Megan's forehead, saying, "You take care of my son and my grandchildren."

Megan stepped back with her eyes wide, speechless.

Cosmo gave Megan a winner's smile, "Call it a grandmother's insurance policy; you conceived the first time you were with Destruction." With that she vanished.

DESTRUCTION SCOOPED MEGAN UP INTO HIS arms and took her to the bedroom. He was in the mood for celebrating.

He had everything he had ever wanted. A woman to love, a woman who loved him back, and now he would get to see his female grow round and full with his child. Suddenly, he paused mid-stride. Not even Megan's lips on his neck could shake of the panic that rushed through him.

"Megan, baby did she just say grandchildren?" He verified she'd heard too.

She paused in her seduction, "Oh my God..... Twins?"

IN THE FOLLOWING DAYS, THEY DECIDED THAT they would live in the human world. Megan had so much to show Troy. She hoped he would learn to love it as much as she did.

His mother had been true to her word. He was able to walk with Megan down the street without leaving destruction in his path.

Megan soothed his soul and made him complete... Tamed.

Megan was right, she had explained to him what he'd never seen before. It was like seeing both sides of the same coin.

On one side, the wreck and ruin of a cyclone, on the flip side, human resilience. After destruction, there is always rebirth; people grow stronger, together.

ABOUT THE AUTHOR

Melissa Bell is a USA Today Best Selling Author who lives in Brisbane, Australia. At a point in her life where she felt she needed something just for herself, she discovered the pleasures of writing. Her most frequently used comment to herself is there's not enough time in a day. She enjoys good food and good company, when she's not trying to concentrate on her writing. She also loves to laugh and most of the time, she cracks herself up. She is hoping that this is the start of something amazing and one day aspires to be listed amongst those blessed with the title of being on the New York Times Best Sellers list.

When she isn't writing she loves to read, many of which she has read over and over again while listening to her favorite Australian bands - Birds of Tokyo and Karnivool.

Please keep an eye out for other books by Melissa Bell.

Stay safe and thank you for reading my book.

Please visit your favorite retailer to discover other

books by Melissa Bell.

Dutiful Gods Series

Book #1 Destiny's Fate

Book #2 Taming Destruction

Book #3 Morpheus's Dream

Book #4 Defying Death

Book #5 Cosmo (TBA)

FIVE BROTHERS SERIES

Book#1 Houston

Book#2 Felan

Book#3 Tate

Book #4 Channon

Book #4.5 Lupe

(First story in 'Compilation'- A Collection of Short Stories)

Book #5 London

Books still to come in this series include –

Blaez and Brody amongst others.

(So stay tuned)